KIDS CAN'T STOP READING
THE CHOOSE YOUR
OWN ADVENTURE® STORIES!

"Choose Your Own Adventure is the best thing that has come along since books themselves."
—Alysha Beyer, age 11

"I didn't read much before, but now I read my Choose Your Own Adventure books almost every night."
—Chris Brogan, age 13

"I love the control I have over what happens next."
—Kosta Efstathiou, age 17

"Choose Your Own Adventure books are so much fun to read and collect—I want them all!"
—Brendan Davin, age 11

And teachers like this series, too:
"We have read and reread, worn thin, loved, loaned, bought for others, and donated to school libraries our Choose Your Own Adventure books."

CHOOSE YOUR OWN ADVENTURE®—
AND MAKE READING MORE FUN!

Bantam Books in the Choose Your Own Adventure® Series
Ask your bookseller for the books you have missed.

INVADERS OF THE PLANET EARTH

BY RICK BRIGHTFIELD

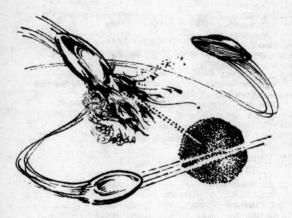

ILLUSTRATED BY LESLIE MORRILL

An Edward Packard Book

BANTAM BOOKS
TORONTO · NEW YORK · LONDON · SYDNEY · AUCKLAND

RL 4, IL age 10 and up

INVADERS OF THE PLANET EARTH
A Bantam Book / August 1987

*CHOOSE YOUR OWN ADVENTURE® is a registered trademark of
Bantam Books, Inc. Registered in U.S. Patent and Trademark
Office and elsewhere.
Original conception of Edward Packard*

*Cover art by Richard Corbin
Inside illustrations by Leslie Morrill*

*All rights reserved.
Copyright © 1987 by Ed Packard.
Cover art and inside illustrations copyright © 1987 by
Bantam Books, Inc.
This book may not be reproduced in whole or in part, by
mimeograph or any other means, without permission.
For information address: Bantam Books, Inc.*

ISBN 0-553-26669-1

Published simultaneously in the United States and Canada

---

*Bantam Books are published by Bantam Books, Inc. Its trade-
mark, consisting of the words "Bantam Books" and the por-
trayal of a rooster, is Registered in U.S. Patent and Trademark
Office and in other countries. Marca Registrada. Bantam
Books, Inc., 666 Fifth Avenue, New York, New York 10103.*

PRINTED IN THE UNITED STATES OF AMERICA

O   0 9 8 7 6 5 4 3 2 1

For Susan Korman

WARNING!!!

Do not read this book straight through from beginning to end! These pages contain many different adventures you may have as you confront the invaders from space. From time to time as you read along you will be asked to make a choice. Your choice may lead to success or disaster.

The adventures you have are a result of your choice. You are responsible because *you* choose! After you make your choice, follow the instructions to see what happens to you next.

Think carefully before you make a decision. Remember: The aliens have the power to destroy the entire Earth! You may be the only one who can save your planet.

Good luck!

This adventure begins in the future, ten years after the Taurons have invaded planet Earth. They came from their star, Tau Ceti, fighting and conquering their way across the galaxy. Now Earth is just one among the hundreds of planets they rule.

The Taurons are not typical conquerors; for the most part they leave Earth's people alone. In fact, though the Earth has survived ten years of Tauron occupation, no one really knows what they look like. Rumors describe them as everything from gorgeous humanoids to slithery little spider-legged creatures. One thing is certain though: Their electronic equipment is highly sensitive to ordinary electrical current—so sensitive that a flashlight beam could destroy one of their ships! To prevent this, the Taurons have decreed that *any* use of electricity will be subject to attack. What this means for Earth is that there are no more airplanes, automobiles, radios, or electric lights.

There have been many attempts to fight the powerful aliens, but none has been successful. Only the Vorks, members of a small star federation, have so far managed to resist the warlike Taurons. But the Vork resistance may not last long. Outside of what was once the city of Denver, Colorado, the Taurons have set up a military outpost designed to help them in their conquest of the Vorks.

Turn to page 2.

2

Recently you've heard rumors that the Taurons are planning to move on. It could just be nonsense or it could be true. One fact is known: The Taurons never leave a planet without totally destroying its civilization.

You don't know how you can stop the Taurons, but you have to try.

Turn to page 4.

You lie there on the floor, stunned. You feel as though you've been run over by a coal wagon. The professor is lying a few feet from you, his clothes smoldering. Lisa manages to crawl over and roll him into a piece of heavy curtain that she pulled from the window. You push yourself to a sitting position and shake your head, trying to get rid of the ringing in your ears.

You all sit there in shock for a few minutes. The ringing in your ears gradually goes away. The professor pulls himself to his feet and staggers to the workbench.

"It worked! It worked!" he exclaims.

"Are you all right?" Lisa asks.

"Fine," he says, and picks up the metal tube gently. "This is the *first* gravbar. Now all I need is someone who will go out and test it against the Taurons. I'd go myself, but I've got to start making more gravbars."

"I'll do it!" you say.

"I can't ask someone I barely know to go out and risk their life with this thing," he answers at once. "Besides, it means going to New Denver— straight into the Tauron outpost!"

You walk over to him and say, "There's no other way. We've got to do it."

The professor sighs; he knows that you're right. A moment later he says, "Hand me the gravbar. I'll show you how it works."

Turn to page 18.

4

From the porch of your house in the small town of Midville, Colorado, you can see the results of the Tauron invasion. Wrecked and rusted automobiles sit uselessly along the side of the street. Overhead, power lines trail from their poles. Long ago they stopped carrying electricity into your home. Telephones, televisions, stereos, and electric lights are things of the past. And it's the same all over the planet. People travel by horse and wagon or bicycle. Trains still run, but only on steam engines. Using anything else, even a flashlight, immediately signals the Taurons. Their ships appear, and within minutes blast apart whatever was turned on. From what you've seen, there's no doubt they could destroy the planet.

As you look down the street you spot your friend Ricky on his bike, coming your way.

"There's a band of jugglers on the village green!" he calls out, skidding to a stop. "Let's go check them out. Maybe they've got some news from Metro or they know something new about the Taurons."

"All right," you call back. "I'll get my bike."

A minute later, you spin around the side of the house, and the two of you ride toward the center of town.

Turn to page 8.

You wait until you're sure the explosions are over, then the three of you cautiously check the window. A column of smoke rises from the top of a tall building in the distance. Above it a Tauron patrol ship circles the smoke and then speeds away.

"Probably some fool with a flashlight," mutters the professor. "Use electricity and the Taurons are here in seconds!"

"Something has to be done about them," you say.

"I intend to do something," the professor replies. "For years I have been working on a new form of power, a force the Taurons will be unable to detect. There is one final step necessary to activate the first *gravbar*. Tonight, I believe I will have the energy needed for that step."

"What step?" you ask, trying to make sense of all this.

"I will need a tremendous charge of electricity," he answers.

"Electricity?" Lisa says. "The Taurons will blast you and this whole place to dust!"

The professor doesn't look nearly as worried as his niece. "There is one type of electricity the Taurons can't control—lightning. We can use its energy against them, and they won't even realize it. And I think tonight is the perfect time!"

"Give me one good reason," Lisa says.

Go on to the next page.

"A storm's coming. I can feel it in my bones. It'll be the perfect chance for the gravbar to charge itself. You see, it attracts lightning the way a magnet attracts iron."

"Is this gravbar in here?" you ask, looking around the barren apartment.

The professor frowns. "Of course not. It's up on the top floor. If you want to help me tonight, I suggest we start up there. Then again, it would be as valuable to me if you got some information about how we can test the gravbar against the Taurons once it's activated."

"How far up is the top floor?" you ask.

"From here? Thirty floors," the professor answers, and starts toward the door.

*If you want to help activate the gravbar,
turn to page 17.*

*If you'd rather search for information,
turn to page 48.*

8

When you reach the village green you find the jugglers in full swing. Nearby a troupe of acrobats is performing a tumbling routine, and a magician is doing card tricks. You and Ricky walk through the crowds, taking it all in.

You haven't gone too far when a familiar voice calls out, "Hey, you two!" It's your friend and neighbor, Lisa. She runs over and says breathlessly, "Guess what! You'll never believe this, but I'm going to Metro to stay with my uncle Mortimer!"

Ricky gives a low whistle. "Metro's a wild place."

"You're lucky to get to the city," you say. "I hear it makes Midville seem totally dull."

"Well, you two could come if you wanted to," Lisa says. "There's plenty of room, and I'm sure it would be all right with my uncle. Besides, it's only for a little while."

"My parents would never let me," Ricky says. "The Taurons have attacked five sites there just this last week."

"I'm not sure," you say, wondering what you'll tell *your* parents. And then something else occurs to you—another rumor. Metro is *supposed* to be the center of a resistance movement against the Taurons. If you're serious about fighting them, it might be a good idea to pack your bags now—before it's too late!

If you decide to set off for Metro with Lisa, turn to page 10.

If you decide to stay in Midville with Ricky, turn to page 64.

You decide to stay in your seat. You put your shoulder bag down underneath it, but you're worried about the gravbar wrapped up inside. You wonder if the man next to you somehow knows about it. You try to shake off the thought and ignore him.

"You are going to New Denver?" the man suddenly asks. His voice has a mechanical sound, and he looks down at you with strange eyes that seem to look right through you.

"Uh . . . yes. Just visiting some relatives," you answer, thinking quickly.

"I see," the man says.

"I had a feeling that your journey might be more important than that," the man says, finally. "It may have something to do with the Taurons—yes? Perhaps we are going there for similar reasons. In that case, we should be friends."

You look closely at the stranger. Why is it that you feel you might be able to trust him? you ask yourself. Still, you have mixed feelings. He could be a Tauron or one of their agents.

If you decide to trust him, turn to page 50.

If you don't trust him, turn to page 58.

"Wait for me," you tell Lisa. "I want to go to Metro with you."

You pedal home as fast as you can and, after assuring your parents that it's okay with Lisa's uncle, you get permission to go. It takes you no time at all to pack and get to the railroad station where Lisa is waiting for you. Together you watch the huge steam engine chug into the station and stop with a loud hiss of steam.

The train ride is great—faster than anything you can remember, and yet you know that before the coming of the Taurons, steam trains were considered so slow that they were no longer used. The conductor tells you that on an electric train the ride between Midville and Metro took twenty minutes.

Nearly two and a half hours later, the steam train pulls into Metro. The sky has clouded over, and as you leave the train, Lisa says, "I hope we can make it to my uncle's place before the rain starts."

You hardly even notice the weather. You're staring at the giant skyscrapers left from the age of electricity. The buildings rise so high you can barely see the sky; but you know that without elevators or plumbing, most can only be used for the first seven or eight floors. And the streets are narrow, crowded with horses pulling wagons and carriages.

Lisa leads you through the downtown area to the base of the tallest skyscraper in Metro. She looks at you and grins. "Get ready to climb some stairs," she says, "because this is the place!"

Turn to page 16.

"I have a secret weapon," you tell Acton. "It throws a beam that can cut holes through walls—and it doesn't use electricity, so the Taurons can't detect it."

"Sounds very useful," Acton says. "We may get a chance to use it tonight. The first attempt on the Tauron base is going to be made by just you and me. Right now, let's get some rest."

As soon as it's dark, you meet Acton on the front porch of the boarding house. You bring the grav-bar with you. Acton knows the way, and you follow him off into the night. After a while, a crescent moon rises and you can see some of the countryside. You follow a narrow trail through low brush and across fields that were probably once farmland.

Suddenly, a harsh voice comes out of the darkness: "Halt! And stand where you are," it commands.

Turn to page 56.

"Don't make a sound!" warns a voice.

You try to sit up straight, but a strong hand forces you back to the ground.

A moment later the voice whispers, "Roll back into the underbrush, but make sure that they don't see you."

You ease back over the pine needles until you are safely hidden behind a tree. A girl about your age is crouching alongside.

"This whole thing is a setup," she says bitterly. "Those guards out there aren't for protection. They're holding us captive."

"I figured that out a while ago," you say, "and as soon as it's dark, I'm off into the woods and gone."

"Perfect," the girl says sarcastically. "Just when the guards are on full alert. Be smart—we can get back into the wagons and wait for a good chance farther down the road."

You consider the possibilities and politely say, "What's your name?"

The girl looks at you and says, "I'll let you know. But for now, you can call me Helen. Now what's it going to be?"

If you decide to slip into the woods, turn to page 54.

If you decide to stay with the wagons, turn to page 67.

The three spinning stars—now turned into expanding balls of purple fire—hang suspended in the air as though they had landed on top of an invisible dome. Crackling veins of brilliant light radiate out from them, and the flame spreads out over the top of what must be a gigantic force-field, arching miles high into the sky.

Moments later the metal posts along the ground explode, throwing out a shower of fragments. You're glad that you are behind the log.

You shield your eyes from the blinding wall of light that rises into the sky a few yards away. You manage to see the sheriff leap to his feet and dash back toward town. You don't see Acton.

Then, from a few feet away, you hear his voice.

"In a few more seconds, all their protective screens will go down," he says. "Then we're going in."

Turn to page 49.

You and Lisa go into the lobby of the building and look at the listing of tenants posted on the wall.

"This is it—Professor Mortimer Cromley, room 1806," Lisa says, reading from the list. "That's on the eighteenth floor."

"You mean we have to walk up eighteen floors!" you exclaim.

"Looks like it," Lisa says. "We might as well get started."

You find the stairwell and climb up and up. Finally, you reach the eighteenth floor. Then you go down a long, wide hallway until you find a sign on a door reading CROMLEY SCIENTIFIC FOUNDATION. Lisa knocks.

The door opens, and there stands a tall, thin, bald-headed man with a small, neat pointed beard.

"Lisa!" he exclaims. "It's so good to see you. And I see that you've brought a friend."

"I hope you don't mind," Lisa says.

"Not at all," Professor Cromley replies. "We've plenty of room. In fact, there are another thirty empty floors above us."

Suddenly, there is a booming explosion outside the building. Everything shakes for a few moments, and you can hear the windows in the next room shatter.

Turn to page 6.

You and Lisa follow the professor up the thirty flights of stairs. Halfway up, you and Lisa have to stop to rest. The professor is the only one who doesn't seem to be tired.

Finally, you reach the top floor. The wide, probably once-luxurious penthouse is strewn from one end to the other with scientific equipment. At the far end is a large workbench. And on it is a metal bar about a foot and a half long and about twice the thickness of a broom handle.

"None of this equipment uses electricity," says the professor. "Except of course for the final activating charge of lightning. This heavy wire runs from the gravbar on the bench to a lightning rod on the roof just above us."

A distant flash lights up the sky outside. This is followed a few seconds later by the rumble of thunder.

"It won't be long now," the professor says gleefully.

The storm soon reaches Metro, and streaks of lightning flash across the sky. Suddenly there is a loud crack and a bright flash of light outside as the lightning strikes the rod on the roof. The heavy wire turns white hot as the electricity surges through it and into the bar on the table. A second later there is a deafening crash, and a blinding explosion fills the room, knocking you all to the floor.

Turn to page 3.

You carefully lift the bar from the workbench. "This end is hollow," the professor says. "Don't try sticking your finger into it or you'll be missing one finger. The other end is smooth and shiny like the sides—except for a small bump in the center. Watch; I'll point the hollow end away from me and press the bump for a second."

As he does, a faint blue beam of light shoots out of the end and over into the wall. A circular hole appears in the wall where the beam hits. You watch in amazement.

Turn to page 24.

"General Claymore's camp is to the south," Helen says.

You can hear the horsemen getting closer, and suddenly you turn to Helen, a suspicion forming in your mind.

"I know what you're thinking," Helen says, "but I really *am* from the general's headquarters. He sent me to find out what was happening to the volunteers that never reached his camp."

The horsemen gallop past you, and you realize she's telling the truth.

"Those guards we escaped from are probably Taurons and—" you start.

"No. I've seen the actual Taurons," Helen interrupts. "The guards are people under their power. The Taurons have ways of controlling people's minds."

"In any case," you continue, "we'll have to get back to Metro and put a stop to this phony recruiting. That's our number one priority."

Helen shakes her head, saying, "You don't know scratch about military procedure. We should head straight for the general's headquarters and tell him exactly what's going on. That's the way it's done!"

She's full of determination, but the choice is yours.

If you want to go back to Metro, turn to page 110.

If you want to head for the general's headquarters, turn to page 69.

"I guess I'll go for the education," you say.

The Taurons barely seem to hear you; they're completely caught up in their own report. "The protective force-field has now been restored. Acton's bomb caused some damage, but that will soon be repaired. A tube of some sort was seen to fall into the flames. If it was also a bomb, it must have melted before it had a chance to go off," says one of the Taurons, giving you a strange look. You are not sure why they are telling you this.

They take you to the education chamber. There a helmet is placed over your head. All of Tauron history starts to flash before your eyes—how they arrived half a million years ago from another galaxy and started to build a system of peace and prosperity throughout this one. Then you see the uprisings of the evil Vorks on rebellious planets, designed to disrupt the Tauron progress.

Go on to the next page.

Twenty minutes later, when they lift the helmet from your head, you are a loyal follower of the Taurons.

"I will do all I can to serve the Tauron forces," you say mechanically.

"We can see from your cerebral profile," one of them says, "that you have exceptional ability and potential. In fact, you are eligible either to be a commander of one of our battlecruisers or to go to our home planet and work for Tauron intelligence."

If you decide to become a commander, turn to page 44.

If you go to their home planet, turn to page 94.

Acton seems to know his way around the inside of the Tauron ship. You follow him as he moves cautiously down a narrow corridor, then through a door into the central control room. A broad panel covered with flashing lights curves under an observation window. Two Taurons are slumped unconscious in swivel chairs in front of it. This is the first time you've actually seen any Taurons in the flesh. You're surprised by how small and thin they are. Their heads are humanlike, but hairless and oversized for their small bodies. They have slanted eyes and thin slits for mouths. They each have two small holes where their noses should be.

Acton says, "The beam from your tube didn't completely penetrate their protective screen, but it did throw the ship out of control. The force of the crash knocked out the pilots. Help me drag them outside, then we'll take a spin in this thing."

You grab one of the Taurons under the shoulders and pull him down the corridor. He is as light as a feather. Just as you and Acton get the pilots outside, two more Tauron ships zip by overhead.

Acton pulls you inside the ship and slams the outside door shut. Then he dashes down the short corridor and jumps to the controls. You are right behind him. You barely have time to squeeze yourself into one of the small seats in front of the control panel before the ship takes off straight up into the air.

Turn to page 75.

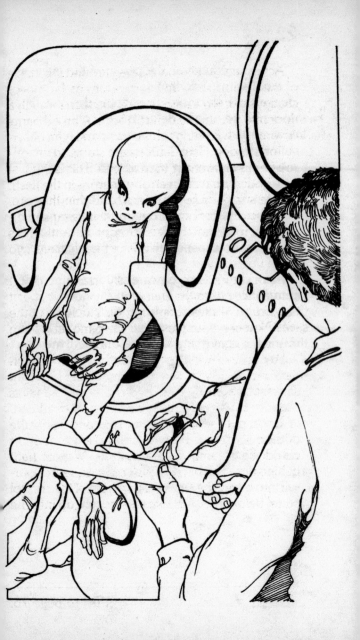

"Now that you know the power of the gravbar, be careful with it," continues the professor. "Since it doesn't use electricity, I'm hoping that the Taurons won't be able to detect it until it's too late— that is, until we put some holes through *them*."

"I'm staying here," Lisa says to her uncle. "You've got a burn on your arm from the explosion, and you haven't even noticed!"

Professor Cromley mutters something about not having time for burns, but somehow you all get back down to the eighteenth floor and into his apartment. You spend the rest of the night sleeping.

The next morning you carefully wrap the gravbar in a piece of cloth. Then you say good-bye to Lisa and the professor and go back down to the street. You're not sure just *how* you're going to test the gravbar against the Taurons, but there must be a way.

Turn to page 34.

The horses break into a full gallop. You reach the edge of the woods just as the Tauron ship returns and hovers over the farmhouse. A beam flashes down from the ship, and with a deafening roar the house explodes in flame.

For a moment, the three of you are fixed by the sight. Then the farmer wheels his horse around, saying, "It doesn't matter. It was only a building."

With that the three of you set out into the night. You travel silently, staying out of sight, hoping that the foliage overhead will hide you from the probing beams of the Taurons.

It is nearly morning when you approach General Claymore's camp. A sentry steps out onto the trail.

"Halt!" the guard orders. "What's the password?"

"The geese are flying," answers the farmer quickly.

The guard nods. "Dismount and go ahead on foot," he says. "I'll tend to the horses."

Turn to page 30.

You join Claymore's forces. The next night a Vork spaceship lands near his headquarters. The ship is shaped like a huge boulder—so different from the sleek Tauron ships. A door opens in the side and several of the Vorks start unloading cases of silvery balls. They look like sets of Christmas tree ornaments. General Claymore is clearly disappointed.

"You expect me to defeat the Taurons with *these*?" he asks the commander of the Vork ship, a man named Klaro.

Klaro laughs, juggling two of the silvery balls in his hands.

"You will see," he says. "Jump aboard my ship and I'll take you to a little demonstration."

You, Helen, and the general go inside the ship and sit on a bench that curves around the side of a circular compartment. You sit there for a few minutes.

"When is this thing taking off?" the general asks impatiently.

"We're already there," Klaro says.

Turn to page 74.

The gypsy caravan travels all night and most of the next day, always remaining within the cover of the forest. Just after sunset, they pull into a clearing, where they arrange their wagons in a circle. You help build a campfire in the center, and Natalia ladles out portions of stew to everyone. It's the same stew you tasted before, and it's still delicious, but this time it doesn't make you dizzy.

Later, when the singing and dancing begins, Natalia comes over and sits beside you.

"There's something I'm curious about," you say. "Do the gypsies have any contact with the Taurons?"

"We are not traitors to Earth," Natalia says defensively. "We have our own way of dealing with the Taurons. Our gypsy magic is all that has kept them from destroying the earth."

"Magic?" you ask.

"Yes," she says. "The Taurons think we are trading herbs from the forest to flavor their food, but actually we are giving them magic potions to make them peaceful."

Go on to the next page.

A man called Carlos comes over and speaks to Natalia in Romany, the gypsy language. Then he turns to you. "We are meeting to trade with the Taurons this very night," he says. "You may come if you wish. But I must warn you, the Taurons can be dangerous. It is always possible that we—and you—will not return from the meeting."

If you want to attend the meeting with the Taurons, turn to page 89.

If you'd rather wait and explore the gypsy camp, turn to page 80.

30

The trail winds along a steep hill and ends at the opening of an old mine shaft. This is General Claymore's base of operations. The general notices your approach and breaks away from his aides.

"What's the situation?" he asks directly.

Helen explains how loyal volunteers are being captured.

The general listens carefully, then says, "Our battle with the Taurons is not far off. We're expecting a shipment of advanced weapons from the Vorks to arrive momentarily. And right now we need every loyal fighter we can get. Those volunteers are critical to our effort."

You take a step forward and ask, "How can I help?"

The general looks you over and says, "If you want to be a hero, you can tackle those monkeys that are capturing the new recruits. Or," he points ahead, "you can join the regular force. Suit yourself, we're all in this mess together."

If you want to take on the false recruiters, turn to page 110.

If you want to join General Claymore's forces, turn to page 27.

A few seconds later, the Tauron patrol ship flies straight into the larger ship and lands at the far end of a huge hangar. The Taurons lead you to a small door in the towering wall at the side of it. This opens into an elevator that takes you past dozens of levels to a broad control room. Here computer consoles are arranged around a large central pit where hundreds of points of light float in the air. Here and there among them, you can see different-colored flashes of light.

"This is a holographic representation of a part of the galaxy," one of the Taurons explains, pointing to the pit. "The flashes indicate battles in progress. Your sun is that tiny dot of light way off to the side there. Fortunately for your planet, your sun is far removed from the major actions."

"Then why are you here?" you ask. "Shouldn't you be over there helping to fight the battles?"

"A good question," says the Tauron. "We were sent here to scout for any of the defeated Vorks who might escape to, or take refuge in, this remote part of the galaxy. But now we have a better solution, and it involves *you*!"

Turn to page 93.

You and your forces rush into the base. You search from one end of it to the other, but you can't find any sign of the Taurons. You end up in the broad plaza at the center of the base, wondering what to do.

You are about to send out runners to find out what happened to Claymore and *his* forces, when you are startled by a loud humming sound overhead. It gets louder and louder, until you can feel its vibrations rippling through your body. Suddenly you and the others find that you can't move. You are frozen into whatever position you happen to be standing in.

A few seconds later, a huge Tauron spaceship lands in the plaza. Dozens of hatches open on the side of it, and hundreds of small Taurons in their shiny spacesuits come pouring out. They carry you and the others—like so many statues—into the ship. There they stack all of you in a large storage compartment.

The ship takes off, speeding away from Earth and into deep space. You have no idea what will happen to you now, but something tells you that it won't be pleasant.

The End

With the gravbar safely in your bag, you head straight to the train station. Stepping up to the ticket counter, you ask for a one-way to New Denver. The ticket agent looks you up and down, then asks in a low voice, "Are you sure you want a one-way to New Denver? That's in the middle of the Tauron zone. It's not much of a town. . . ."

"Yes, that's exactly what I—"

"But you . . ." the agent continues, ". . . hardly no one goes there anymore. There's just not that much reason to. You can't even get a—"

"Look," you say, tapping on the counter. "I don't want you to plan my trip. Just sell me the ticket."

"Well, sure," says the agent. "We can sell you a ticket . . . now, let's see . . . that was New Denver . . . correct?"

When the transaction is finally complete, you slip the ticket into your pocket and head out to the platform. The next train leaves in about an hour. As you pace back and forth, you notice that the thin man at the other end of the platform seems a bit too curious about your activity. Whenever you look over, his eyes slide back to his newspaper, but so far he hasn't turned a page.

Go on to the next page.

Soon the train pulls in. You climb aboard and take a seat next to the window. A few moments later, the thin man enters the far end of the car, works his way toward you, then sits down by your side.

If you want to keep your seat, turn to page 9.

If you want to get up and head for the next car, turn to page 97.

Acton tries to point his small weapon at the craft overhead, but he suddenly lets out a cry and drops it. You can see the weapon glowing red hot on the ground. Could the beam from above be doing something to it? you wonder. If it is, luckily it's not affecting the professor's gravbar. Almost without thinking, you aim the bar upward and press the bump on the end. A glowing, pale-blue beam shoots upward and hits the underside of the Tauron ship. For a few seconds nothing happens, and then you hear a sudden loud metallic whine overhead, and the ship begins to wobble violently. Seconds later it plummets sideways and smashes into the ground nearby.

"Let's go over and take a look," Acton says, slowly getting to his feet. "Be careful and keep that tube of yours handy."

One side of the Tauron ship is dug into the ground, but the ship seems somehow undamaged. Acton walks around the outside examining it. Then he presses a spot on the hull and a door slides open. He stands there for a few moments listening.

"I don't hear anything," he says. "The ship is undamaged, but the Taurons inside may be dead or unconscious. I'm going in to take a look. You can come inside with me or stay here and stand guard with your tube. I expect more Tauron ships will arrive at any moment."

If you enter the Tauron ship, turn to page 22.

If you stand guard outside, turn to page 79.

Electric beams, but that's impossible—the Taurons would be here in no time! Unless . . . several hands reach down and drag you and Helen out of the ditch . . . unless they're already here!

"Don't let the others know what's happening!" the man from the restaurant orders. "Take them by the alternate route."

You and Helen are tied up and tossed into the back of a small cart. It jostles and bumps along a narrow trail through the woods. There is no sign of any other wagons.

At dawn you enter a narrow valley. Waiting there is a Tauron ship. The empty wagons of the original group are drawn up on one side. The volunteers, their hands tied behind their backs, are being herded onto the ship.

"This is how it ends," says Helen, peering through the slats of the wagon. "Forced into Tauron slavery."

Not necessarily, you think to yourself. Once on board, we can band together, organize a revolt . . . take over the ship. These ideas race through your head, but suddenly, they're overridden by a powerful Tauron voice that fills your mind.

"Your thoughts of rebellion will not be tolerated. They will stop at this time."

As soon as you realize that the Taurons have been monitoring your mind, the wagon you're in is engulfed in a powerful beam of light. When it fades nothing is left.

And *that* is how it all ends.

The End

You direct your forces to fan out on both sides of the central part of the Tauron base, but not to get too close. Then, off in the distance, you hear explosions. There must be a battle going on there, no doubt between the Taurons and Claymore's men.

It's clear that you have to create a diversion to draw the Tauron forces away. Quickly you order your group to set their grenades at maximum force and hurl them at the base. A series of terrific explosions rips through the nearest buildings. This starts a chain reaction and the whole base, from one end to the other, erupts into flame.

Overhead a formation of Tauron ships retreats from the battle with Claymore. They circle the flaming base, then suddenly spiral up into the sky and disappear into a huge mother ship.

As the Tauron base continues to burn, Klaro arrives in his strange-looking spaceship.

"They've pulled out," you announce, "but I expect that any moment they'll blast apart the earth!"

Klaro looks to the sky and says, "Not a chance. The Taurons need all of their firepower to defend themselves against the Vork armada that's heading this way. And I'll bet that as we speak they're zipping into deep space as fast as they can."

You laugh to yourself. Klaro's news almost makes you feel like going out to buy an extension cord—just so you'll be ready when the power comes on!

The End

The Vorks take you back aboveground. A door opens in the side of one of the boulders, which are actually disguised Vorkian spaceships. Once the ship lifts off, you're amazed to discover that you can't feel any motion or even vibration. There is just a slight low-pitched hum. During the flight, which you guess takes several days, the Vorks put you in a small, private room where you watch videotapes of life on the Vorkian planets. Every so often, shorter programs come on showing Tauron atrocities throughout the galaxy.

Voltan, the training planet of the Vorks, turns out to be almost completely covered with jungle. There are recruits of all sizes and shapes there from across the galaxy, some of them humanoid, others very strange looking. Most of the training consists of learning how to blow things up, particularly with silvery grenadelike weapons and small star-shaped bombs. After a few weeks pass you begin to have doubts about all this and about the Vorks themselves. Is all this destruction necessary to free the galaxy from the Taurons? you wonder. And what will the Vorks do if they win and they take over?

Turn to page 106.

You're put aboard one of the Vorkian ships, and the craft takes off. The flight is smooth and quiet. Things seem to be going pretty well. But half an hour later the ship rocks to the side and starts shaking violently. Something is happening, but you're locked up in a small room and can't be sure of what it is.

On the other side of the metal door you can hear the crew members shouting. The ship banks hard to the side. Suddenly you put things together— the cruiser is under attack!

There's an explosion somewhere on one of the other decks. And then another hits, this one closer. A few seconds later you're thrown across the room. You didn't even hear that one, it was so close. Maybe you were knocked out. There's no way of telling. You don't remember.

Sometime later everything goes still. The power has been cut. The lights have dimmed. Then from the other side of the door to your room you hear the sound of ripping metal.

Turn to page 96.

You start up the stairway to the higher floors of the abandoned skyscraper. You have no idea how many floors there are, but there sure are a lot. You keep going up. Every few floors, you stop to catch your breath. Down below you, you can hear heavy footsteps racing up the stairs. If you keep going, you think, maybe they'll give up. No such luck! The men keep coming after you, and they're getting closer.

Then you see a large bin on one of the landings. You just have time to climb inside. A few seconds later the two men, puffing hard, reach the landing. They stop and listen.

"Is . . . this . . . really necessary?" one of them asks in gasps. "This . . . person . . . we're after may not suspect anything."

"We can't take any chances," says the other man in a cold, hard voice. "Not with what the Taurons are paying us."

Unfortunately, the bin that you are in is very dusty, and you suddenly sneeze.

Turn to page 91.

You arrive at the Tauron command school to be trained to command a battlecruiser. The Taurons use the whole planet of Sentar—instead of their home planet of Sarm—as a school for officers and pilots.

You sit for hours with a training helmet on your head. The helmet electronically feeds all the details of such subjects as astrophysics and advanced Tauron weaponry into your head—without you having to memorize anything or even think. The facts are mechanically implanted in your brain so that you will never forget any of them.

In two weeks your training is completed. You are given a fancy uniform covered with gold braid, and at a formal ceremony, you are appointed to the rank of battlecruiser commander.

Things happen fast in these advanced societies, and two *days* later you're given a battlecruiser to command. Immediately you are ordered to travel into the active battle zone. On arrival you find that your sector is heavily occupied by Vork spaceships. Within moments you are under full attack!

Turn to page 73.

The Vorks give you a course in all the latest technology of the galaxy. You learn about sub-space and hyperspace communication, as well as the most effective galactic weapons and transport systems. The studying is hard; you have to spend eight to ten hours a day at it.

"We used to use learning helmets," explains one of the Vorks, "but we found that to really understand a subject, you have to learn it the hard way."

Finally, you finish your course with high marks. You are now considered a full-fledged Vorkian agent. The Vorks assign you to work at night in the same secret underground complex where you did your studies. Every day one of their strange-look-ing ships takes you home just before dawn and picks you up just after dark.

A few months later you recruit your friend Ricky as a new Vorkian agent, and he goes through the same rigorous training that you did. Together, you work with the Vorks to track secretly the move-ment of the Tauron ships in the sector near your sun.

The work is dangerous. The slightest mistake can prove deadly. Worst of all, everything must be kept secret. You can tell no one about your mis-sion. Not your friends, not even your family! But you still never want to give it up. And the reason is quite simple: When it comes to being a sly spy . . . you're the best!

The End

Just to make *sure* that you don't do anything against them, the Taurons fasten a bracelet around your ankle that monitors your activities.

"Don't try to take this off," one of the Taurons advises. "It is filled with explosives. They'll go off if you try."

Then they take you in one of their patrol ships to the outskirts of Midville. Unfortunately, several people see you getting off their ship. You try to walk into town, but before you've gotten far, an angry crowd has formed around you accusing you of being a Tauron spy.

"I'm not a spy!" you holler. "I was captured by the Taurons."

You show them the ring on your ankle and tell them why it's there. Finally, they believe you and let you go home to your family.

Fifteen years go by before the Taurons are finally forced to leave the earth. You still aren't able to remove the Tauron ring from your ankle. You realize that for the rest of your life, somewhere in the galaxy, someone will always be monitoring your activities.

The End

"I'll see what I can find," you tell the professor.

"Good. I'll have the first gravbar ready when you get back," he replies. "Lisa is going to stay here and help me."

"Terrific," Lisa groans.

You go back down to the street. Where can I start? you ask yourself. You've heard a lot about the Taurons, but mostly guesses and rumors. No one in Midville had ever seen one or even a picture of one.

For almost an hour you wander through the city of Metro. The streets that were so crowded when you arrived now seem deserted.

Finally, you see a sign for a restaurant up ahead. Who knows—maybe these Taurons hang out in public places. In any case, you could use a meal. So you pull open the door and step inside.

The restaurant isn't crowded. You buy some food at a counter and take it to a dimly lighted booth at the back of the large dining room. You are sitting there quietly, eating your food, when you hear whispered voices in the next booth. They are talking about the Taurons!

Turn to page 72.

A few seconds later the immense dome of light blinks out. Except for the pale moonlight the Tauron base is completely dark.

"I hope *all* their sensors are out," Acton says. "Those stars were designed to start a chain reaction that penetrates and knocks out all their defenses, but one never knows."

You follow Acton between what's left of the posts—a few jagged pieces of metal sticking out of the ground. Acton moves with an animal's stealth. He holds a small gunlike device in his hand.

You go on cautiously for an hour or so. When you finally see a pattern of lights clumped together and hugging the horizon far up ahead, Acton pulls you down. A Tauron patrol ship whizzes by close to the ground. The ship passes, then stops in mid-air and comes back. A searchlight beam shines down below it, catching you and Acton in its circle of light.

Turn to page 36.

"I *would* like to do something about the Taurons," you say. "But what can—"

"We cannot talk here," the man says. "When we get to New Denver, we will talk."

You still have mixed feelings about trusting him, but now at least you don't feel quite so alone. Aside from telling you that his name is Acton, the man doesn't say much for the rest of the trip.

The train arrives in New Denver early in the morning. The town looks like pictures you've seen of frontier towns in the Old West. Two-story wooden buildings line the gravel-covered streets. A row of horsedrawn carriages is tied up just outside the train station.

Acton seems to know where he is going. You follow him off of the train and over to the carriages. Together you take one to a boarding house at the edge of town. There you register for separate rooms, then take a table in the corner of the small restaurant on the ground floor.

"We can talk freely now," Acton says. "The people here are fighting the Taurons just as you are. Tonight we will attack the Tauron base. The Taurons are completely blind in the dark. Unless they have the light of their ships they cannot see without extremely bright light. They come from a planet with three suns where there is never any night."

Go on to the next page.

"You know a lot about the Taurons," you say.

"One must know one's enemy," Acton says. "You see, they destroyed most of my planet—the planet Zanar. And we Zanarians are just one of many peoples fighting the Taurons. They call us Vorks."

"I'll do anything I can to help," you say.

"We are greatly outnumbered, and our mission will be difficult," Acton says. "The Tauron base is well protected. But tonight, I'll show you a few tricks we Vorks have learned."

You decide to tell Acton about the gravbar that you have in your bag.

Turn to page 12.

You and Lisa wait across the street and watch the restaurant. Whenever someone comes out one of you follows and explains about the phony recruiters. During the rest of the day you manage to brief several dozen people one by one.

That evening all the supposed recruits meet behind the restaurant. Unsuspecting the three recruiters show up. They are in for a surprise.

Instead of the recruits getting into the wagons, they seize the three men and tie them up. Then they haul them off to the Metro police.

You and Lisa are proud of yourselves for a day's work well done. You hope that you'll have as much luck fighting the Taurons. Now that you have the gravbar, with more on the way from the professor, you and your fellow Earthlings have a fighting chance.

Many adventures lie ahead of you—and you will win out in the end, though not exactly in the way you think.

The End

54

You and Helen creep away from the camp and into the woods. Moving quickly and quietly, you disappear into the underbrush. It's dark and tangled; you can barely see the ground. While climbing over a fallen log you lose your footing. Helen reaches out, but it's too late. Head over heels, you both go tumbling down a steep ravine.

When you reach the bottom your heart is pounding and your arms are scratched, but around you the woods are all quiet.

"I think we're all right," Helen whispers.

Just then a powerful beam stabs through the darkness. . . . You're trapped in the light!

Turn to page 37.

You carefully open the back door of the gypsy wagon and slide out. Fortunately, the wagon is going very slowly. The trees brush against it as it goes along the narrow trail. You have no trouble slipping into the woods.

You quickly make your way through the dark forest until you can no longer hear the gypsy wagons bumping down the trail. Then you slow down to a fast walk. You hope that you're heading toward Midville, but in the darkness it's impossible to tell. For over an hour you continue on through the forest.

Finally, the trees thin, and you come to a grassy clearing. You blink in amazement as you look around. There are a dozen large, almost identical boulders evenly spaced around the sides of the clearing. It looks a bit spooky, to say the least. But you are tired, and you can't face the idea of going back into the forest.

Wondering what to do next, you sit down on the ground and lean back on one of the boulders. The boulder seems to move ever so slightly as you do. But it must be your imagination. These boulders are enormous.

You start to doze off. Your eyes close and you drift into a pleasant dream of what the earth was like before the loss of electricity. Then, half in your dream, you hear a loud crackling sound. You wake up with a start. When you open your eyes, what you see makes you jump to your feet with fright.

Turn to page 71.

56

In the dim light, you can see a stocky figure holding a shotgun blocking the trail.

"Just where do you think you're going?" a deep voice demands. "You're about to blunder into the Tauron force-field and be annihilated. So turn yourselves around and head back the other way."

"I'm afraid we can't do that, sheriff," Acton says calmly. "You see, we're here to fight the Taurons."

"Fight the Taurons!" the sheriff exclaims. "You must be crazy! They'll wipe you out in a second."

"There's always that chance," Acton says. "But I think I have something that will stop them. Will you help us?"

The sheriff hesitates. Finally, he says, "I must be as crazy as you are. Tell me what I can do."

"Lead us to the edge of the Tauron force-field and I'll show you," Acton says.

You follow the sheriff to where a line of six-foot-high metal posts are set in the ground about thirty feet apart.

"Step between those posts and you're hamburger," the sheriff says.

From a pouch on his belt Acton takes out three small, flat, star-shaped objects. He hands one to you and one to the sheriff and keeps one himself. They are very heavy, considering their small size.

Go on to the next page.

"Each of you go off to one side about a hundred paces," Acton says. "When you hear my whistle, throw your star as high and as far over into the force-field as you can. Then run from the poles and hit the ground!"

You go off to the side. When you hear the whistle you throw your star with all your might. It's so heavy that you expect it to go only a short distance. Instead, once it leaves your hand, it spins high up into the air, leaving a streak of light behind it. You run for a few seconds and dive behind a log.

Turn to page 15.

58

The man next to you sits rigidly upright as the train rumbles along the tracks.

You sit there in silence for a long time.

"My name is Acton," he says finally. "Isn't there something you would like to tell me?"

You try to ignore this question. Then you pretend that you are asleep.

As the train pulls into the station in New Denver, Acton suddenly grabs you by the wrist. His grip is like iron and his hand is as cold as ice.

Turn to page 90.

You still have the rest of the evening—before going to see the general—to look for more information for the professor. You continue to search the city, but you don't find anything.

About an hour after dark, a violent thunderstorm breaks out. You see several lightning bolts strike the top of the building where the professor lives. You hope that his experiment is successful and that he and Lisa are all right.

It has stopped raining by midnight, and you find the alley behind the restaurant. There a small crowd of volunteers is climbing aboard a row of wagons. You climb into one of the wagons yourself. Then they start off through the back streets and are soon on a country road outside the city. The wagons travel all night. At the first pale light of dawn, they pull off of the road and into a grove of pine trees.

"We'll eat and rest here for the day," one of the men from the restaurant announces. "As soon as it's dark, we'll start off again. Right now, we have special guards protecting us from any kind of attack."

What kind of attack? you wonder. From the Taurons? You begin to have doubts about this whole thing.

You find a shady spot in the woods where the pine needles form a thick carpet, and lie down. But you have a hard time falling asleep.

Some time later you feel a hand roughly shaking you awake.

Turn to page 13.

The Taurons have a patrol ship take you back to the outskirts of Midville, and you walk home from there, carefully carrying the box.

Your parents are very glad to see you back safely. You don't tell them about the box—after all, you promised to keep it secret.

The next day, the people on Earth find that the Taurons have gone. It starts the task of restoring electric power and service. No one but you knows that it's all possible because of the small box you have sitting on your shelf—next to the television and the radio.

The End

62

You tumble through space. Suddenly a beam of some sort from below catches you and stops you in mid-air. You're glad not to be falling anymore, but you find it hard to breathe. You gasp for air as you lose consciousness.

When you come to, you are in a room lying on a low table—and surrounded by Taurons.

"So good of you to drop in on us," one of them says. Could it be that the Taurons have a sense of humor? you wonder.

"Acton has somehow managed to escape us again," says another. "We identified him from the voice tapes taken from the wreckage of the patrol craft that you fell from. He obviously deceived you. You had no way of knowing that he is a dangerous terrorist. So dangerous that the High Council once considered destroying this whole planet just to be rid of him."

"Knowing Acton," says the first Tauron, "he's already deep in space. His small ship has eluded our detectors before."

You look around angrily. "Why don't you all head out into deep space?" you ask. "Then you could devote all of your time to looking for Acton and leave us alone to get on with things."

Go on to the next page.

"You are an inferior life form," says the Tauron. "We have saved your race from certain destruction by the Vorks and probable destruction by yourselves. You would do well to learn from us. If you think that is possible, I offer you the chance to use one of our educating machines. It is very effective, but we will not force you to use it. If you choose not to, you may simply return to your own kind. . . . We only require that you not engage in anti-Tauron activities . . . *Ever*."

You think it over. An easy education or a free ride home . . . There *must* be a catch.

If you decide to use the Tauron educating machine, turn to page 20.

If you want the free ride home, turn to page 46.

You're heading back home, when Ricky says, "Let's swing past the old farm and see if the gypsies are still camped there."

"I've seen them before," you say, not very interested.

"Yeah, but don't forget those rumors that they sell herbs to the Taurons," says Ricky. "Let's check it out."

A little way out of town, where the road swings close to a stream, you find the gypsy camp.

You and Ricky get off of your bikes and walk over. The gypsies are seated in a wide circle. In its center, two dancers whirl to the rhythm of guitars and tambourines. One of the gypsies comes over and offers you some of the dark stew that the others are eating. It is a mixture of meat, vegetables, and herbs that is delicious. It also makes you thirsty. Another gypsy offers you something to drink. As soon as you drink the pale, bubbling liquid, your head starts to swim. Even though you know you aren't moving, you feel as if you are spinning around with the music, first floating up into the air—then down into a dark whirlpool as you lose consciousness.

Turn to page 102.

You turn your ship sharply to the right, trying to avoid the attack of the enemy ships. As you do, the beams from the Vorkian ships catch yours broadside, ripping it open from one end to the other. You barely have time to scramble into your personal lifepod and blast free before your battlecruiser disintegrates completely.

The Vorks have the Tauron fleet on the run. The battle swirls away through space. Soon you are alone in your tiny lifepod, drifting aimlessly in a vast, deserted section of space. Since you have no way of telling how long it will take you to be rescued, you put yourself into suspended animation.

A year later, the alarm in your pod wakes you. Down below you can see the surface of a planet, and your pod is coming in for a landing on automatic pilot. Unfortunately, as you will soon discover, you're landing on the dark, dangerous, and forbidding planet of Nulcar, sometimes called the Planet of the Dragons. Nulcar has been devastated and depopulated by the huge dragonlike creatures that arrived from space eons before.

You *may* be able to help the few surviving Derns, members of the race of small, gentle hominids that once prospered on this planet, to fight these creatures. *If* you can defeat the dragons, you will live out your life as the greatest hero of Nulcar and the liberator of the Derns.

The End

You and Helen are the last ones to get onto the wagon, so you are sitting at the back. It starts off into the darkness. Following Helen's signal, you wait for a couple of hours, then you both carefully slip over the back railing and drop to the ground. The next wagon in line is far enough behind to give you time to slip into the woods. You go a short distance and then crawl under some bushes, lying there quietly as the wagon train goes by. The last wagon is followed by a group of men on horseback—some of the guards. You can see their silhouettes against the bright stars overhead as they go by. Fortunately, they don't suspect that you are missing.

After they've gone past you turn to Helen. "Who is this General Claymore?" you ask.

"A veteran of the war my grandfather fought in," she replies. "And our only hope against the Taurons. Now come on!"

You follow her deeper into the forest. You're just beginning to believe you've lost them, when you hear shouting coming from the direction of the wagon train.

"I think they've discovered that we're gone," you say.

Helen turns pale but says briskly, "Those horsemen will be looking for us. We'll have to move fast and get as far away as we can."

You find a narrow trail and run along it for what seems like an hour. Finally, you sink down on the ground, exhausted.

Turn to page 19.

You walk to the edge of town. You see a small boy playing at the side of the road. You ask him if he's heard of the Tauron base.

"Sure I have," he says. "It's down that path over there. But I wouldn't go near it. My parents told me if I went there I wouldn't come back."

You thank the boy for the information and head down the path toward the base. The boy watches you go, scratching his head.

You walk for what seems like hours. Finally, you come to a row of metal posts. A sign in front of them says:

BEWARE TAURON BARRIER
DEADLY

Another sign with a skull and crossbones is nearby.

You experimentally toss a rock between two of the posts. It immediately flashes into flame. No doubt about it, the Taurons don't want anyone to get onto their base. You sit there for a while wondering what to do. You don't notice someone coming up behind you. At the last moment, you notice him and try to turn—but it's too late.

Turn to page 115.

When you've caught your breath you both head for General Claymore's camp. You know that the agents of the Taurons are after you. Occasionally, you hear shouts and whistled signals in the woods—sometimes far away but sometimes dangerously close.

"If they catch us, it's all over," you say.

"I know," Helen agrees. "There's a farm not too far from here. The farmer is one of our supporters. He'll be able to help us."

You set off at a trot along the edge of a field. The moon has risen, and before too long the farmhouse comes into view. Cautiously, you circle up to it. Everything looks quiet. Helen approaches the front door and knocks twice. A moment later the door swings open, and a large man stands framed in the light.

"They're after us," says Helen quickly.

The man looks around, then says, "I have horses in the back. Come this way."

You go around to the stable and mount up. Just at that moment a Tauron patrol ship looms overhead.

"Quick!" the man shouts, "we'll head for the woods!"

Turn to page 25.

All of the boulders are hovering just above the ground. There is something very wrong here. You are turning to run back into the woods, when a large trapdoor in the center of the clearing opens. A tall figure rises silently from beneath the ground.

"Do not be afraid, earthling," the figure says. "I am a Vork. We are here to help you fight the Taurons. Come, I will show you."

He beckons you to follow him, and you realize that you no longer want to run. You walk forward almost as if you were in a trance.

Turn to page 78.

"General Claymore is having trouble raising an army to fight the Taurons," one of them whispers. "He needs more volunteers."

"I'll try to get as many as I can," another man whispers back.

"We'll leave for the general's camp at midnight from behind the restaurant," says a third man.

You poke your head around the corner of the booth.

"I might volunteer," you say.

There is silence for a few seconds as the three men look at you with shocked expressions.

"I'm not a Tauron spy or anything," you say. "If there is such a thing as a Tauron spy."

"Oh, there is," says one of the men. "You can be sure of that. But we'll take a chance and trust you. If you overheard our conversation, you know that we're leaving for the general's camp at midnight. If you'd like to come along as a volunteer, you're welcome."

These men are a little too careless discussing their plans. It could be some kind of trap, you think. And you are supposed to be getting information for the professor. But if these men are on the level, the general might be able to give you some useful information.

If you decide to go to the general's camp, turn to page 60.

If you decide to stay in Metro City and continue to look for information, turn to page 84.

You're standing in the control room of your battle cruiser. A formation of Vork ships is closing in. They open fire, but their lasers are off the mark.

You turn to your first officer and say, "Issue battle alert. Prepare all decks."

Just then a Vork blast rips into your ship.

"We took a good one that time!" one of the Taurons under your command reports to you with a shaky voice. "The Vorks are directly behind us and somehow getting shots through our defensive screens."

You climb into your chair in front of the console. Then through the front viewport you see several more enemy ships bearing down on you from a different direction.

"Awaiting your command," says your chief lieutenant nervously.

You have to do something quickly.

If you turn your ship to meet the attack head-on, turn to page 105.

If you veer sharply to the right to avoid the attack, turn to page 66.

The door opens, and you all go outside. The moon is up again, and you can see that you are at the edge of a wide clearing. Klaro leads you to its center, where he takes out a small, battery-powered flashlight and turns it on. You shiver, knowing that the Taurons will probably be here in a matter of seconds. Klaro calmly puts the flashlight on the ground and places one of the silvery balls next to it.

"Now, let's get back to the trees," Klaro says.

You get there just as a Tauron ship arrives and hovers directly over the spot where Klaro left the flashlight and the ball. A beam shoots straight down from the ship. A fraction of a second later a streak of light shoots up from the ground, and the Tauron ship explodes with a tremendous blast. Soon there is nothing left of it except a cloud of tiny glowing particles drifting slowly to the ground.

"You see," Klaro says, "the silver grenades are attracted to the source of the Tauron beams."

The general smiles. "This may be exactly what we've been waiting for!" he says. "Let's give it a try."

You all get back aboard Klaro's ship and return to the camp.

Turn to page 92.

You grit your teeth and hold on to the side of the chair. You look fearfully out of the observation window in front of you. It's the first time you've been off of the ground. Far off to the left—in the direction of New Denver—you see a string of dim lights; they must be the oil lamps in the homes there. Below to the right is a brilliantly lit circular complex of buildings and machinery. Those were the bright lights you saw in the distance when you were on the ground.

"Their defensive shields are still down," Acton says. "If we can get directly over the core of the Tauron base, we can deliver a few more exploding stars. Hold on! I'm going to try."

The ship moves sideways so suddenly that it throws you out of the chair.

"There's a hatch behind you that will open if you press the lever there on the side," Acton continues. "Be careful you're not on top of the hatch when you do it."

You see the lever. You press it and you are suddenly looking through a hole into space.

"Toss this out when I tell you," Acton says, sliding one of the star-shaped bombs over to you.

"Now!" he shouts.

Turn to page 81.

You climb up on the railing between the train cars and jump! The steam train is going faster than you realized, and you tumble forward heavily onto the adjacent set of railroad tracks.

As the train that you just left rolls by, you look up and see the man's face pressed to a window. His mouth is open as if he is shouting something.

You are about to try to get to your feet, when a train coming from the opposite direction slams into you. It knocks you ten feet into the air and into oblivion.

The End

The Vork leads you underground into a vast complex of rooms filled with a strange collection of tubes and ducts.

"This is our underground base," he explains. "From here we are able to coordinate our war against the Taurons." He turns to you and says, "We have the technology. We have the knowledge. We can train you as an agent. . . . You will be very effective against the Taurons."

You raise your eyebrows to show that you're interested.

The Vork continues, "You will be well paid for your service, and while it will at times be quite dangerous, I promise that it will also be very exciting."

He pauses while you look around at the equipment, then says, "This complex is very complete. It meets all the requirements for an installation of this type. But it is not as sophisticated as the unit on the planet Vork. . . . Though I should caution you, the flavor of our planet may be a bit too . . . exotic for your taste. I'll give you a moment to consider."

If you want to travel to the Vork planet for training, turn to page 40.

If you'd rather train on your home planet, turn to page 45.

Acton carefully enters the Tauron ship. A few minutes later, you hear it try to start up, making a series of grinding noises. You wonder if it's Acton or some surviving Taurons operating the ship. Then the ship starts to hum. At the same time, a flight of Tauron ships zips by overhead. The ship with Acton aboard takes off—it goes straight up so fast that it just seems to vanish. You watch as points of light zigzag across the sky, several in pursuit of what must be Acton's ship.

There is suddenly a crackling sound all around you. What feel like electric shocks start to run up your legs. At the same time, a terrible pain starts in your head. You try to run, but fall to the ground. It feels like your head is going to explode. You realize to your horror that the Taurons must have their deadly force-field back in operation.

The last thing you feel is a tremendous jolt of Tauron current streaking through your body.

The End

Later that night, you watch as Carlos and Natalia start off into the forest on their way to meet with the Taurons. As soon as they have left, you start to wish you had gone with them.

The rest of the gypsies are sitting around what's left of the campfire, singing and humming softly to themselves. You sit off by yourself on the side gazing up at the sky. Suddenly you notice that large sections of the stars are being blotted out by large, black shapes. At first you think that they are some kind of strange clouds, but then you realize that they are falling straight down out of the sky. They settle on the ground in a wide circle around the gypsy camp.

Turn to page 112.

You drop the star through the hatch. At the same moment a beam from one of the other Tauron ships slams into yours. The shock knocks you forward through the hole, and the gravbar flies into space. Frantically, you grab for something. You manage to catch the edge of the hatch with one hand and hold on for a few seconds while the exploding star goes off with a brilliant flash below you. Then another blast hits the ship, tearing you loose. You plummet downward into the inferno caused by the bomb.

Turn to page 62.

The last man running slides to a stop. He turns around and says, "You could do a lot of damage with that thing . . . especially considering all the explosives that are stored downstairs."

With that, he tosses a lighted match down into the basement and then dives out into the alley.

There's no time to think. There's no time to run. And what's even worse . . . about the explosives . . . that guy wasn't kidding!

The End

"I *would* like to meet the general some time," you say. "But right now I'm busy with something else."

You leave the restaurant and head down the street. You haven't gone far when you get a funny feeling. You don't know exactly why, but you think you're being followed. You duck into a doorway and wait. No one comes after you. After a while, you start feeling foolish. You go out and start down the street again. As you are walking along, you catch a reflection in a piece of polished metal projecting from the front of a building. You see two men at the other end of the block coming in your direction. They look like two of the men from the restaurant, but they are too far away for you to be sure.

You start walking faster. You take a quick glance behind you and see the two men hurrying in your direction. Quickly you duck into the lobby of an abandoned skyscraper. At the other side of the lobby are two stairway signs. One says, TO THE BASEMENT, the other one simply says, UP. You have to make a quick decision; the men are not far behind you.

If you go up, turn to page 43.

If you go down to the basement, turn to page 98.

The Vorks force all of you into one of their spaceships, which is what the dark shapes turn out to be. You are made to sit on the floor of a featureless circular room. You sit there for hours. Finally, one of the Vorks comes in.

"We have arrived at a secret iridium mining complex on the planet Zarkan," he announces. "You will all remain here until you have been permanently assigned to our system."

You and the gypsies are forced to slave in the mines for several months. They work you day and night and permit you very little sleep and food. You are completely exhausted and have all but given up hope of ever escaping from the mines. Then one day the supervisor of the mines has you sent up to his office.

"I must say that I'm quite impressed with your work here. You are doing a fine job," he says. "That's why I'm sending you to one of the home planets of the Vorks to continue your good work."

"What kind of work? Mining?" you ask warily.

"I'm not at liberty to say," he says. "But I can tell you that the work will be . . . ah, similar."

Turn to page 41.

You say good-bye to Natalia and Carlos and step into the Tauron ship. The door to the outside closes with an ominous thunk.

"The commander of *Expedition Earth* would like to speak to you himself," says one of the Taurons in a high, toneless voice.

You are directed to a small, metal chair. As soon as you are seated the ship takes off straight up into the sky. You can see out of the viewport that it's heading for a large, glowing object high above.

As you get closer to it you see that the pale moonlight is shining off the silvery surface of a huge, cigar-shaped ship. Soon, it completely fills the viewport in front of you. A large door is opening in its side, no doubt for the patrol craft you are in to enter.

Turn to page 31.

At the first light of dawn your band of fighters spreads out along the wall of the Tauron force-field. You have carefully calculated the timing and intensity of the special grenades to ensure that the protective shield is destroyed.

Your fighters distribute the devices according to plan. At your signal the timing mechanisms on the charges are activated. You have twenty-five seconds to clear out! Running fast and low over the rough ground, your band races away to take cover among the jagged rocks.

Just as you dive for cover a deafening blast rips through the air. The ground trembles and shakes from the power of the explosion. You look behind. The force-field is splitting apart—it looks like a shattering mirror!

The dust is still in the air when you lead your band back into the central core of the Tauron base. It is strangely quiet. There is no sign of activity. Nothing moves.

"I don't understand it," says Helen. "Have they pulled out?"

You look around at the complex of buildings. Should you go deeper into the fortress or hold your position until General Claymore's forces arrive?

*If you want to go deeper into the base,
turn to page 33.*

*If you want to wait for Claymore's forces,
turn to page 38.*

Later, when the campfire has burned down low, you set out with Natalia and Carlos along a narrow forest trail leading away from the gypsy camp. After a while, you come to a high, barren hill rising out of the trees.

"We will wait here until they come," Carlos says.

The wait is not long. High up, you see a whirling circle of flashing lights. As the Tauron ship descends, you can just barely make out its silvery hull against the night sky. It floats slowly and silently down, landing gently at the top of the hill.

A port opens in the side, throwing a bright finger of light into the night. Three small silhouettes appear in the door. One of them gestures for you all to come up the hill. As you get closer you see that the Taurons look like small children dressed in silver foil Halloween ghost costumes. Carlos gives them a small package and they give him one in return.

You are about to start back down the hill, when one of the Taurons leaves the ship and comes up to you.

"We would like you to come with us for a short time," the Tauron says, offering no explanation. "We will not harm you in any way."

"If you don't want to go with them, we'll try to get you out of here," Carlos whispers to you.

If you agree to hear what the Taurons have to say, turn to page 86.

If you don't trust the Taurons, turn to page 107.

"This is your last chance," Acton says. "You must—"

With all your strength, you pull your arm free and dash off the train. You race down the streets of New Denver, not even knowing where you are going. You turn one corner and then another, hoping to shake Acton for good.

Finally, out of breath, you stop in a narrow alley between rows of two-story wooden buildings. There is no sign of Acton. Now you have to decide what you are going to do next.

If you decide to lay low in town,
turn to page 108.

If you head for the edge of town to try to find
the Tauron base, turn to page 68.

The two men run over to where you are hiding.

"Aha, we've got you," says the man with the hard voice, pulling out an old-fashioned revolver.

Shaking, you grit your teeth and wait for the shot.

Suddenly a pencil-thin beam shoots out of the darkness from the other end of a hallway branching off of the landing, catching the man with the gun in the back. He screams and fires wildly, several bullets going through the bin where you are hiding. Then he sinks to the floor. The other man dives for cover behind the metal post at the top of the stairway, but he overshoots his mark and goes tumbling down the stairway, landing at the bottom with a sickening thud.

The Vork who tried to save you runs over and looks in the bin where you are hiding. But it's too late. One of the bullets got you right between the eyes.

The End

The next few days are a whirlwind of activity, as Klaro supervises the training of General Claymore's forces. The small silvery balls turn out to be more than just simple grenades. A set of buttons on each one can program the grenade for a wide range of things, from disrupting the Tauron force-fields—the invisible walls that are as tough as solid steel—to blasting their ships out of the air. You do so well in the training that General Claymore gives you a small band of fighters to lead.

Finally, the general calls everyone together and gives a speech: "Our efforts tomorrow may determine the fate of the earth and its peoples—slavery or freedom!"

Everyone lets out a cheer. Even if you don't defeat the Taurons, you feel, at least you are fighting back with all you've got.

Early the next morning, a few hours before dawn, your small army marches over empty, barren land toward the Tauron base.

When you are almost there, the forces split up. The main group under General Claymore marches to one side of the huge base while a smaller force under your command, goes to the other side. Your band is to attack first, to knock down the protective force-field on the outer perimeter and to create a diversion so that the force under Claymore can follow up with an attack on the core of the Tauron base.

Turn to page 87.

"Me?" you say.

"Yes," replies another Tauron, standing behind you. "I am the commander of this expedition and I propose giving you a device that you must keep absolutely secret. To outside observers it will look like an ordinary small box. But if any Vork ships try to flee into this sector, the box will respond with a flashing red light and a low beeping sound. Then you will open a small door in the side and press the yellow button. This will alert our forces by way of a hyperspace communications relay. If you promise to do this, we will evacuate our forces from your planet."

"Will we get our electricity back?" you ask.

"Most certainly," says the commander.

"Then I'll do it," you promise.

Turn to page 61.

The Taurons take you to the main city of Tlanth on their home planet of Sarm. At first you're fascinated by all you see. Since the Taurons themselves are so small, everything seems to be in miniature. The buildings in the countryside surrounding the city are like doll houses. The city itself is composed of tiny buildings that look like oversized chess pieces placed on an endless chessboard. And there are fabulous creatures there from all over the galaxy. Some resemble lobsters, others are more like snakes, but except for the Taurons themselves, none resembles a human.

After a while you start getting homesick for Earth. The ceilings in most of the Tauron buildings are so low that you are forever hitting your head. The Tauron planet has three suns, arranged in the sky so that it never gets dark. The light is so bright that you have to wear special glasses to protect your eyes. There are no sunrises or sunsets, and the sky is a never-changing brilliant orange.

You are proud to be a loyal follower of the Taurons, but the work they give you is boring—keeping records of all the people who don't like the Taurons, which include most of the inhabitants of the galaxy.

But you'd better get used to it. You're going to be here for a long time.

The End

The door flies open. Five Taurons stand before you, their ray guns leveled at your head.

"A prisoner," says the tallest, whose head just about reaches your shoulder. At once the Taurons lower their guns. "This ship has been abandoned by the Vorks and is now nothing more than a derelict in space," he continues. "Any prisoner of the Vorks is a friend of ours. We will see that you return to your home planet safely."

You can hardly believe it, but as promised, the Taurons take you back to Earth, setting you down just outside Midville. You are so grateful to them for saving your life that you vow to tell people how they helped you. You write several letters to the local newspapers explaining that even the Taurons have their good side. This doesn't make you very popular in Midville, but you've been through enough not to care.

The End

You ease out of your seat and without looking back, hurry forward—all the way into the next car. You take a quick look back and see that the tall, thin man is coming after you a car behind.

You keep going and come out into the space between the next two cars, where just a railing separates you from the outside. The train is still moving slowly enough to let you jump off.

If you jump off, turn to page 77.

If you stay on the train and wait to see what happens, turn to page 101.

You dash down to the basement of the sky-scraper. It's dark, very dark, down there. You feel your way along into the maze of passageways. They twist and turn and are filled with all sorts of pipes and abandoned machinery. You go deeper and deeper into the maze, trying to get away from the two men that you know are after you.

Finally, you stop and listen. You can't hear anything except the sound of dripping water somewhere. Just to be sure that the men have given up looking for you, you wait for about an hour. Then you start trying to find your way out again. But you just keep going around in circles. You are completely lost.

Many hours later, you sit in the darkness wondering if you will ever find your way out.

The End

You walk straight into the restaurant. Those three phony guys are back. They don't look surprised to see you. And that's a bad sign.

One of them gets up from the table and at the same time pulls a pistol out from his coat. You dive over the counter as several shots are fired.

The next second Lisa bursts through the door. A pale beam shoots down the length of the diner, blowing out the back wall. The blast knocks the three men off their feet, but a second later, they're up and running out the back.

You leap over the counter yelling, "Don't let them get away!"

Lisa points the gravbar like a shotgun and yells, "Freeze!"

Turn to page 82.

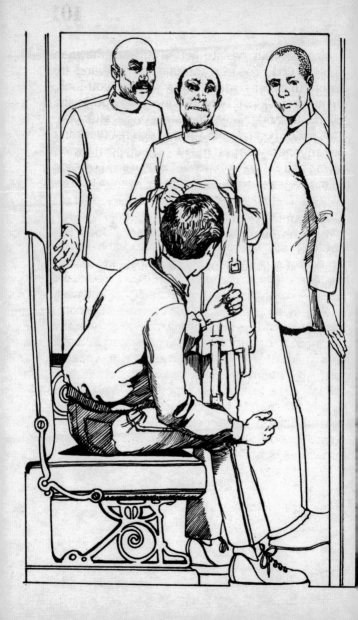

You do your best to get away from the man chasing you. You run through the cars and try hiding under the seats. But whenever you look, there he is—close behind. Finally you go to the conductor and tell him that someone is after you.

"I noticed you running up and down, but I didn't see anyone coming after you," says the conductor, giving you a suspicious look. "Why don't you hide in the baggage compartment until we get to New Denver. I'll lock you in."

That sounds like a good idea, but once you are locked in, you start to get nervous and wish you could get out again. You are about to start banging on the door, but then you realize that here at least you are safe from the man chasing you. You make yourself comfortable sitting on a suitcase and wait.

When you get to New Denver, you hear a commotion outside your compartment. When the door finally opens, several men dressed in white are waiting for you. They put a white coat on *you*—backward and with straps.

"We get a lot of these types these days," says one of the men to the conductor. "They all think that the Taurons, or sometimes the Vorks, are after them. A good rest at the sanitarium and they are usually all right."

The End

You wake up with a headache inside a moving wagon—a gypsy wagon.

"What am I doing here?" you ask, pulling yourself upright.

"Do not be afraid," says a gentle girl's voice. "I have been waiting for you to wake up."

"But how did—" you start.

"You must have many questions," the girl interrupts. "I will try to answer them after you have some coffee."

The girl lifts a pot from a brazier in the corner and pours you a cup.

"My name is Natalia," she says as she hands it to you. "You wanted to come with us, so we brought you."

"What?" you say, trying to put your thoughts together.

"You sent your friend—what was his name?—ah, Ricky, that's it—to tell your family you would be gone for a while," Natalia says.

"I did? Really?" you say.

"Continue to rest. I will be back soon," Natalia says as she slips out of a door at the end of the wagon.

Go on to the next page.

You look out of the curtained window. Night has fallen. You're traveling down a narrow dirt road through the forest.

You're not sure if you asked to come on this ride, but you know darn well you didn't send Ricky off somewhere. That girl's story is seriously off. The smart move would be to head back to Midville, and right now. But still, there's something curious about this gypsy thing. Why did Natalia lie to you?

If you want to stay with the gypsies to see what develops, turn to page 28.

If you'd rather skip out and head for Midville, turn to page 55.

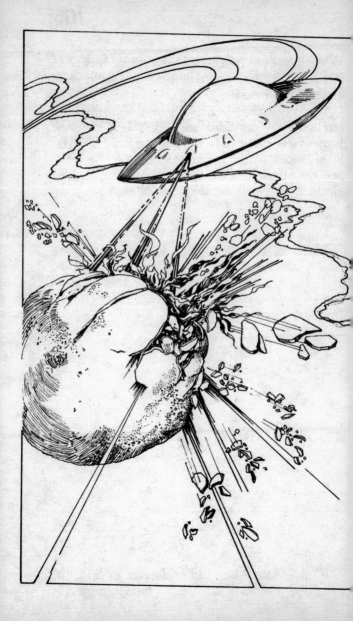

You press the buttons on the console in front of you that will turn the ship head-on to the attacking Vorkian ships. A second later, you give the order to fire. An array of deadly lasers shoot out from your ship. Caught by surprise, the enemy flies directly into them. You watch as their ships disintegrate and become fireballs in space. Your last remaining human emotion gives a twinge of doubt—how could you have done this?

"Commander!" a voice comes in over the intercom. "The other Vork ships are retreating!"

"Excellent," you reply, all doubt gone.

Later, when you return to base, you are given a hero's welcome. You are credited with turning back the Vork attack and awarded the highest medal of the Tauron Empire. You are very happy in your new world.

The End

"I think each planet should be able to rule itself without any outside interference," you finally tell one of your Vork instructors.

"But if the Vorks are not there to protect it and tell its people what to do . . ." the Vork starts.

After a while you stop trying to reason with them.

At the end of the course, they fail you. But at least they take you back to Earth and Midville.

Then and there you make up your mind that you're not going to help either side. You realize that the Vorks will probably be almost as bad as the Taurons if they take over.

The End

"I'm not going with you!" you tell the Taurons.

"We think you will come whether you want to or not," replies their leader, pointing a gunlike device at your head.

Instantly Carlos pushes you aside—knocking you out of the way a fraction of a second before the paralyzing beam of the Tauron weapon shoots out. He and Natalia dive the other way.

The Taurons are known for being unable to see in the dark, and even though they crisscross the sides of the hill with their beams, none of you are hit. Finally they give up and fly off in their ship.

You, Natalia, and Carlos regroup at the bottom of the hill.

"That didn't do much for your relations with the Taurons," you say. "I hope I didn't mess things up."

"We've had enough of the Taurons anyway," Carlos says. "From now on we'll direct our strongest magic at them—to make them leave this planet altogether."

You all go back to the camp. As the sun rises, Carlos and the other gypsies begin chanting.

"It is the start of our spell," Natalia tells you. "Exactly three days from now the Taurons will leave the Earth."

You don't quite believe her, but you're willing to give it a try. So you join the circle of gypsy magic, vowing to work with them until the earth has been set free.

The End

You seem to be near the center of town. The main thing you want to do right now is to get away from Acton, and then later find your way to the Tauron base. But you also realize that it's been hours since you've eaten. You see a small restaurant up ahead. It looks safe enough, but still you enter very cautiously. You go in and order a sandwich.

Then, as luck would have it, Acton walks in the front door. You drop your sandwich and, still holding on to your bag, run for the back door of the restaurant.

You never make it. Two men who were sitting at the counter take off after you. One of them tackles you, and another pins your arms to the floor.

Acton comes over and takes your traveling bag. "Here it is," he says to the others, pulling out the professor's gravbar. "This may be useful to us in our struggle with the Taurons."

"But I'm against the Taurons too!" you protest.

"You may well be," says Acton, "but we can't take any chances."

They tie you up and carry you down to the basement. You're not sure how Acton could have known about the gravbar—can he read minds? But then he'd know that you are also against the Taurons.

Whatever the explanation, Acton and his associates keep you prisoner for a long time. You only hope that the gravbar is really being used to fight the Taurons.

The End

110

You say good-bye to Helen and set off for Metro City. There, the first thing you do is look for the building where professor Cromley lives. You find it and climb the eighteen flights again. The professor and Lisa are very glad to see you.

"We've perfected the first gravbar, Lisa and I," the professor says gleefully. "It was activated by the lightning, but from now on it will work on its own. It's even more effective than I had hoped."

The gravbar is a shiny tube about a foot and a half long. It is hollow on one end and has a button on the other. Lisa demonstrates it by pointing the bar at an inch-thick piece of iron set up on the table. She cradles the gravbar on her arm and presses the button. A pale blue beam shoots out of the hollow end of the gravbar and cuts a neat round hole in the iron.

"Wow!" you say. "Once we're armed with these, the Taurons won't stand a chance. But right now we've got more trouble. There's a gang of phony recruiters that's been luring people into a trap." You quickly explain the situation to Lisa and her uncle.

"Let's see what we can do," Lisa says.

Go on to the next page.

The professor hesitates a moment, then says, "But take the first gravbar. You may need it."

You and Lisa race down to the street and head straight for the restaurant used by the phony recruiters.

"I'm going inside," you say boldly. "Cover me with the gravbar."

You take a step toward the door, when Lisa says, "Wait a second. You don't know what you're walking into. Let's wait out here and question whoever comes out."

If you decide to go straight inside,
turn to page 99.

If you'd rather wait and see who comes out,
turn to page 53.

You see flashes of dim light on the sides of the huge shapes as if doors were being opened. Then a few seconds later tall figures with dimly glowing eyes appear out of the darkness. The gypsies jump to their feet, some with knives in their hands. But the figures have ray guns that they aim at the gypsies' weapons. The gypsies cry out in pain, dropping their suddenly superheated knives. The figures force you and all the gypsies into a circle in the center of the camp.

"You have been trading with our enemies, the Taurons," one of the figures announces in a loud, mechanical voice, "therefore we take you into custody in the name of the Vorkian Federation."

"No! Stop!" you cry, stepping forward. "I'm much against the Taurons as anybody, and—"

A small device in the hand of one of the Vorks sends out a pencil-thin beam that strikes you in the arm. A terrible pain runs through your whole body. Your arm feels as if it's been hit by a sledgehammer. You grab your arm and stagger back into the crowd of gypsies.

Turn to page 85.

Someone very strong grabs you from behind. Your arms are pulled behind you and handcuffs snapped on your wrists. Then you are spun around.

It's a sheriff. You can tell from his clothes and the badge on his chest.

"So you're another of those darn fools who come out here to throw rocks at the Tauron fence!" he shouts. "You think you can make the Taurons go away by throwing rocks at them?"

"No, I—" you start.

"You want one of them Tauron ships to zip over here and fry you with one of their fryin' beams?"

You try to explain, but all of your protests are useless. Leaving your bag with the gravbar in it lying in the bushes, he drags you off to the local jail. You are thrown into a small, dark cell.

"You'll stay here until someone comes to bail you out," the sheriff says. "Or pay the fine for reckless rock throwing."

A month later, your family finally hears about your plight and they come to get you, paying the sheriff your fine.

Before you go back home, you go and look for the gravbar, but it's no longer there. But you are still determined to fight the Taurons. And you will fight them until someday, they are finally driven off of the earth.

The End

ABOUT THE AUTHOR

RICHARD BRIGHTFIELD is a graduate of Johns Hopkins University, where he studied biology, psychology, and archaeology. For many years he worked as a graphic designer at Columbia University. He has written *The Deadly Shadow, Secret of the Pyramids, The Curse of Batterslea Hall, The Phantom Submarine, The Dragons' Den*, and *The Secret Treasure of Tibet* in the Choose Your Own Adventure® series and six books in Bantam's Escape series. In addition Mr. Brightfield has coauthored more than a dozen game books with his wife, Glory. The Brightfields and their daughter, Savitri, live in Gardiner, New York.

ABOUT THE ILLUSTRATOR

LESLIE MORRILL is a designer and illustrator whose work has won him numerous awards. He has illustrated over thirty books for children, including the Bantam Classic edition of *The Wind in the Willows*. Mr. Morrill has illustrated *Indian Trail, Attack of the Monster Plants, The Owl Tree, Sand Castle*, in the Skylark Choose Your Own Adventure series, and *Lost on the Amazon* and *Mountain Survival* in the Choose Your Own Adventure series. Mr. Morrill is also the illustrator of the first book in Bantam's Super Adventure series, *Journey to the Year 3000*.

Go On A Super Adventure in a Terrifying New World in the First Choose/Adventure® Superadventure!

January 14, 3000. You've been hibernating in a space capsule for a thousand years. Now you're awake and ready to return to the Earth of the future—but your computer has horrifying news to report. An evil tyrant named Styx Mori has proclaimed himself Supreme Emperor of Earth. He has agents everywhere—even on other planets. And no matter where you land, you face capture—and even death!

This Super Adventure has more—more of everything you like best about Bantam's Choose Your Own Adventure series! It's got more choices, more danger, more adventure—it's the biggest and best CYOA yet!

☐ *JOURNEY TO THE YEAR 3000: CYOA SUPER ADVENTURE #1 26157-6 $2.95 ($3.50 in Canada)*

Buy them at your local bookseller or use this convenient coupon for ordering.

Prices and availability subject to change without notice.

Bantam Books, Inc., Dept. AV2, 414 East Golf Road, Des Plaines, Ill. 60016

Please send me the books I have checked above. I am enclosing $_____ (please add $1.50 to cover postage and handling.) Send check or money order—no cash or C.O.D.s please.

Mr/Ms _____

Address _____

City/State _____ Zip _____

AV2—7/87

Please allow four to six weeks for delivery. This offer expires 1/88.

CHOOSE YOUR OWN ADVENTURE

☐	26252	MOUNTAIN SURVIVAL #28	$2.25
☐	26308	TROUBLE ON PLANET EARTH #29	$2.25
☐	26374	THE CURSE OF BATTERSLEA HALL #30	$2.25
☐	26185	VAMPIRE EXPRESS #31	$2.25
☐	25764	TREASURE DIVER #32	$2.25
☐	25918	THE DRAGON'S DEN #33	$2.25
☐	24344	THE MYSTERY OF HIGHLAND CREST #34	$1.95
☐	25961	JOURNEY TO STONEHENGE #35	$2.25
☐	24522	THE SECRET TREASURE OF TIBET #36	$1.95
☐	25778	WAR WITH THE EVIL POWER MASTER #37	$2.25
☐	25818	SUPERCOMPUTER #39	$2.25
☐	26265	THE THRONE OF ZEUS #40	$2.25
☐	26062	SEARCH FOR MOUNTAIN GORILLAS #41	$2.25
☐	26313	THE MYSTERY OF ECHO LODGE #42	$2.25
☐	26522	GRAND CANYON ODYSSEY #43	$2.25
☐	24892	THE MYSTERY OF URA SENKE #44	$1.95
☐	26386	YOU ARE A SHARK #45	$2.25
☐	24991	THE DEADLY SHADOW #46	$1.95
☐	26388	OUTLAWS OF SHERWOOD FOREST #47	$2.25
☐	25134	SPY FOR GEORGE WASHINGTON #48	$1.95
☐	25177	DANGER AT ANCHOR MINE #49	$1.95
☐	25296	RETURN TO THE CAVE OF TIME #50	$1.95
☐	25242	MAGIC OF THE UNICORN #51	$2.25
☐	25488	GHOST HUNTER #52	$2.25
☐	25489	CASE OF THE SILK KING #53	$2.25
☐	25490	FOREST OF FEAR #54	$2.25
☐	25491	TRUMPET OF TERROR #55	$2.25
☐	25861	ENCHANTED KINGDOM #56	$2.25
☐	25741	THE ANTIMATTER FORMULA #57	$2.25
☐	25813	STATUE OF LIBERTY ADVENTURE #58	$2.25
☐	25885	TERROR ISLAND #59	$2.25
☐	25941	VANISHED! #60	$2.25
☐	26169	BEYOND ESCAPE! #61	$2.25
☐	26040	SUGARCANE ISLAND #62	$2.25
☐	26270	MYSTERY OF THE SECRET ROOM #63	$2.25
☐	26197	VOLCANO #64	$2.25
☐	26291	MARDI GRAS MYSTERY #65	$2.25
☐	26484	THE SECRET OF NINJA #66	$2.25
☐	26471	SEASIDE MYSTERY #67	$2.25
☐	26529	SECRET OF THE SUN GOD #68	$2.25
☐	26653	ROCK & ROLL MYSTERY #69	$2.25

Prices and availability subject to change without notice.

Bantam Books, Inc., Dept. AV, 414 East Golf Road, Des Plaines, Ill. 60016

Please send me the books I have checked above. I am enclosing $_____ (please add $1.50 to cover postage and handling). Send check or money order —no cash or C.O.D.s please.

Mr/Mrs/Miss _____

Address _____

City _____ State/Zip _____

AV—7/87

Please allow four to six weeks for delivery. This offer expires 1/88.

VARSITY COACH

The all-new, action-packed Sports Series that will keep you cheering, page after page!

- ☐ 26033   FOURTH & GOAL #1
  Tommy Hallowell $2.50
- ☐ 26209   TAKEDOWN #2
  Leigh Franklin $2.50
- ☐ 26330   OUT OF BOUNDS #3
  Tommy Hallowell $2.50
- ☐ 26526   DOUBLE PLAY #4
  Lance Franklin $2.50

Look for them at your local bookstore, or use this handy coupon for ordering:

Bantam Books, Inc., Dept. CO, 414 East Golf Road, Des Plaines, Ill. 60016

Please send me _____ copies of the books I have checked. I am enclosing $_____. (Please add $1.50 to cover postage and handling.) Send check or money order—no cash or C.O.D.s please.

Mr/Ms _____

Address _____

City/State _____ Zip _____

CO—6/87

Please allow four to six weeks for delivery. This offer expires 12/87. Prices and availability subject to change without notice.